Enid Blyton ™
Magic in the Playroom

Illustrated by Pam Storey

Illustrations copyright © 1997 Grandreams Ltd
This edition published 2002
© Robert Frederick Ltd., 4 North Parade, Bath
Printed in China

The toys in the playroom were very friendly with the little folk who lived in the garden. There were fairies and pixies, gnomes and brownies, all merry and happy and friendly.

Sometimes the gnomes came to drink a cup of tea in the dolls' house. Sometimes the pixies came to dance to the music of the little musical box.

And sometimes the fairies or the brownies came to play hide-and-seek with the toys.

They did have fun and the toys always loved to see the pretty heads of the little folk peeping over the window sill. But when a family of goblins came to live in the old oak tree in the garden the toys were not quite so pleased to see them.

"The goblins are not so polite as the fairies," said the pink rabbit, shaking his head.

"The goblins have rather bad manners," said the big doll.

"They make a noise when they eat," said the red-haired doll, who was very particular indeed.

But nobody said anything rude to the goblins and each night they popped in at the window with the other little folk.

Then a horrid thing happened. One night, after the little folk had gone back to the garden, the pink rabbit put his hand up to his collar and found that the little brooch which kept his coat together at the neck was quite gone!

"I believe I saw it peeping out of the pocket of one of the goblins," said the clockwork mouse suddenly.

There was a deep silence. The

toys were too shocked for words. To think that one of their guests would steal something!

"You must be wrong, Mouse," said the pink rabbit at last. "My brooch must have dropped somewhere."

So they hunted for it, but it could not be found. "We will not say anything about it at all," said the rabbit. "It is horrid to think that anyone would steal from us."

But after that other things began to go! The red-haired doll missed her necklace! She usually kept it in the kitchen cupboard in the dolls' house – and one night when she went to put it on, it was not in the cupboard! Oh dear!

And worse than that, the walking duck lost her key! It was always kept on a ribbon, tied to her neck, so that it should not be lost. It was easy to wind up the walking duck when she had her key handy like that. But now it was gone! Someone had cut her ribbon in half and taken the key, perhaps when she was playing a game and was too excited to notice.

The toys stared at one another in dismay. Something really must be done now! There was no doubt at all that those bad-tempered little goblins had taken their things.

"We will complain to the others," said the walking duck. "Surely the fairies, the pixies, the brownies and the gnomes will be able to make the goblins give back to us all the things they have stolen!"

So that night the rabbit took Ringding the fairy, Twinks the pixie, Frisk the brownie and Snip the gnome into the kitchen of the dolls' house and shut the door.

"Whatever is the matter?" asked Ringding in alarm, looking at the rabbit's solemn face. "You look as if you have lost a new penny and found a button!"

"I've something to tell you," said the rabbit, "and I don't want the goblins to hear me. Little folk, I am sorry to say that the goblins have been stealing some of our things."

The little folk stared at the pink rabbit in horror. Could it really be true? Ringding went very red indeed. She felt quite cross.

"I don't believe it," she said. "You must have made a mistake, Rabbit."

But when the rabbit told her about his brooch and the red-haired doll's necklace and the walking duck's key, the little folk nodded their heads.

"Yes," said Twinks the pixie. "I believe you, Rabbit. It was only yesterday that I noticed the goblins had a new front door key fitting their lock in the oak tree – and now I come to think of it, it was exactly like the key belonging to the walking duck!"

"What shall we do about it?" asked Frisk the brownie.

"We shall have to use some magic on the goblins," said Snip the gnome. "We must make them give up the stolen things somehow."

"But the goblins know more magic than we do," said Ringding. "Whatever spell we do to make them give back what they have stolen will be of no use – for the goblins know much stronger spells than we do!"

"Well, we will try, anyway," said Snip.

So that night, when the goblins had all gone from the playroom into the garden, the little folk went to the oak tree where the goblin family lived and made a spell to force them to give up the stolen goods. But it was no use at all! The goblins put their heads out of their little windows and laughed at them.

"You don't know enough magic!" they shouted. "Stop your silly spells, or we will make a stronger one and turn you into ladybirds!"

The little folk went away. They didn't want to be turned into ladybirds! They told the toys what had happened and everyone was very sad.

The next night the goblins visited the playroom bold as ever – and do you know, although the toys kept a close watch on them to make sure they did not take anything, those clever goblins managed to steal quite a lot of things.

"Look!" cried the walking duck, peeping into Mummy's work-basket, which she had left in the corner on the floor. "Mummy's little scissors are gone – the ones that she cuts button holes with!"

"And all her needles!" cried the pink rabbit,

seeing the needle-case quite empty.

"And her nice steel thimble," cried the clockwork mouse. "Oh, whatever will she say?"

"It is time we did some magic!" said the rabbit suddenly. "I believe I know how to get back the stolen things. Yes, I believe I do!"

He ran to the toy cupboard and pulled out a big magnet that the children sometimes played with. He and the toys slipped out of the window and ran to the oak tree. They banged on the door and, when the goblins opened it, the toys crowded inside.

"Goblins," said the rabbit sternly, "we have come to get back all the things you stole tonight! We have some wonderful magic, much stronger than any you know! Watch!"

The rabbit took the big magnet, which he had been holding behind him, and showed it to the goblins. They laughed scornfully.

"That will not find anything!" they said.

The rabbit held out the magnet and then a very strange thing happened. The stolen pair of scissors, which had been hidden under the carpet, suddenly flew up to the magnet and hung on the end of it! Then dozens of needles appeared and flew to the magnet, too! They hung there tightly. And then from a goblin's pocket the thimble flew out and rushed to the magnet as well.

"Aha!" said the rabbit, pleased. "You see what a powerful magic we keep in the playroom, Goblins!"

The goblins turned pale, as they stared in surprise. They had never seen a magnet before and they were full of fear. They rushed to the door, crowded out and disappeared into the night.

"We shan't see them again," said the rabbit, pleased. "Let's just look round and see if we can find anything else they stole."

They hunted around and found all the things they had missed and a few more, too! The walking duck took her key from the front door of the oak tree and tied it on to a new ribbon round her neck. She was very pleased to have it back again.

Then back they all went to the playroom and put the needles, thimble and scissors into the work-basket. They laughed whenever they thought of the goblins' astonishment.

"That magnet was a fine idea," said the pink rabbit, putting it away in the cupboard. "I don't think the goblins will rob toys again. They will be too much afraid of magic in the playroom!"